"Ben Ehrenreich's *Hold Still* is a lyrical meditation on grief, attachment, and family—particularly on his mother, American author and political activist Barbara Ehrenreich, and her death—and on the essential wandering into and out of dreams and stories that gives way to a contemplative, at times surreal, attention to plant and animal life and to the world's ongoing violence and turmoil, all set against a backdrop of caregiving undertaken to keep his family close—fed, nurtured, and held—and to understand how they are seen and known in their intimacies and freedoms. These pages offer 'a quiet room, some calm and secret cave, a place to rest without retreating,' and more: a calm that reckons with grief and with the desire to move in and out of the rooms and pages we mourn, even as we try to console ourselves with the stories we need to make true. I'm struck by how delicately Ehrenreich writes about everyday duties and the bewilderment of living in such a time of shared strain."

—Prageeta Sharma, author of *Grief Sequence*

"This is a book one reads again and again. Ehrenreich's rendition of grief literature is as porous and wistful as it is private and dignified. *Hold Still* is unpretentious, even seemingly effortless, yet it weaves together intricate threads of stories, metaphors, and quips into one glorious punchline after the next. By the final page, you can't help but turn back to the first."

—Mohammed el-Ku

Perfect Victims: A

I0894182

"*Hold Still* is at once a refusal of numbness and a capture of the very rich texture of daily life. A small family, a city street, oatmeal, king tides, avian flu, the death of a parent. Shot through with grief and affection, it's an example of how one might reclaim time and fully inhabit it. Ben Ehrenreich is a wonderful writer."

—Chris Kraus, author of *The Four Spent the Day Together*

"*Hold Still* arrives like an IBEW crew rolling up to restore power for whole neighborhoods. Maybe you didn't realize how long everything's gone dark. Ben Ehrenreich uses grief here as a lever, revealing the electric and the extraordinary in the ordinary, sharing daily moments in the light of their own transparent brilliance. This astonishing book's not some jittery or tired buzz—we needed this jolt stronger than juice. Here, *Hold Still*."

—Sesshu Foster, author of *Atomik Aztex*

"*Hold Still* churns and resonates as a narrative in fragments—stories as vaults for mourning and contemplation, memory, and observation. The quotidian veers into the fanciful, the horrific, and back again. Grief charges Ehrenreich's rotation through hectic airports; slow, lumbering bus rides; and rainy walks. Birds of all kinds take turns animating the novel's shifting emotional landscape. *Hold Still* draws its extraordinary power from a pair of whirlwinds: Ehrenreich's late mother; and his young daughter—the latter's heartrendingly concrete 'toddler priorities' laying out the stakes here on earth."

—Grace Krilanovich, author of *Acid Green Velvet*

"The miniature stories in *Hold Still* are dazzling and painful, restless, and sometimes absurd—but above all they are directly and unflinchingly human. They circle around grief and melancholy, exploring in an unvarnished way what it means to lose a parent while living on with a child of your own. *Hold Still* is a quiet, potent book."

—Brian Evenson, author of *Good Night, Sleep Tight*

Hold Still

Ben Ehrenreich

CITY LIGHTS BOOKS
SAN FRANCISCO

HOLD STILL

Cover design by Gerilyn Attebery
Text design by Patrick Barber

ISBN 978-0-87286-947-9

Library of Congress Cataloging-in-Publication Data is on file.

City Lights Books are published at the City Lights Bookstore
261 Columbus Avenue, San Francisco, CA 94133
citylights.com

Special thanks to Adam G. and to the other
Adam G., and to Olivia W., always

When you have arrived at the thing itself,
then all you can do is compare it to something
else you don't understand. A rock. A crow.
The only things that remain themselves
are the ones you can never reach.

—ANNE DE MARCKEN

Contents

Not long after the death of my mother in the fall of 2022, I set myself the task of writing a story every day. I kept at it for a few months, until I didn't want to anymore. I did not expect to share or publish the stories I wrote, or even to read them once they were done. It was, I suppose, a way of saying kaddish, the Jewish prayer recited after a loved one dies. The traditional prayer does not mention death. It praises god, and asks for peace and nothing more. Its repetition maintains a connection between the mourner and the divine, and hence between the mourner and the world. It is through stories that I know how to connect to the world, so I wrote stories.

1

A CHILD FOUND a treasure and hid it in a box. Should I tell you what it was? Maybe not yet. The child left the box under a tree and ran off. A crow watched from the branch above. When the child was gone, the bird flew down and opened the box with its beak. This is not hard for a crow. Not at all. They are smart. But the crow was disappointed. There was nothing to eat inside the box, and nothing shiny or pretty to steal back to its nest. Only a feather, and a crow's feather at that, a sleek, black, ordinary thing. To a crow at least. Annoyed, the crow flew off, and as it did the lid of the box slid shut, catching one of the bird's tail feathers. It squawked out a curse and kept flying.

The next day, or perhaps the day after that, the child returned, kneeled before the box, and opened it. Her eyes went wide as quarters. In the box was not one perfect sleek, black feather but two! The box was magic. Or the feather was. Or maybe the tree. But the child could not linger.

Somewhere dinner was waiting. She closed the lid of the box, opened it again for one more peek, then darted off. This time a magpie was watching from a branch above. As soon as the child was gone, the magpie fluttered down and opened the box with its beak. For a magpie this is not difficult. They are smart. But the magpie, too, was disappointed. There was nothing to eat in the box and nothing shiny, nothing precious. Only two feathers, and crow's feathers at that, sleek and black and worse than ordinary. To a magpie at least. The magpie, disgusted, flew off in a huff. As it did, the lid of the box slammed shut, catching two of the bird's long tail feathers. The magpie groaned out a curse and kept flying.

The very next day, or maybe the day after that, or the next one, but as soon as she could, you can be sure, the child rushed back and kneeled in the leaves at the base of the tree. The box was still there. Eyes squeezed shut, almost afraid of what she would see, the child opened first the lid and then her eyes. What treasure did she find? Not one feather, not two feathers, but four feathers, the first two sleek and black, the others black on one side and on the other a luminous blue, blazed with a badge of pure white across the middle. The box was truly magic! The child didn't wait this time but closed the lid, held the box to her chest, and rushed home.

On the branch above, a peacock, a flamingo, and a macaw sat watching. What do you think she had in that box? asked the macaw. I don't know but it must have been something good, said the flamingo. Too bad, said the peacock, fanning out its brilliant tail. We'll never know.

2

A BOY RAN alone through a burning forest. A bear ran after him. When the boy was at last too tired to take another step, he stopped. The bear, no less exhausted, stopped just behind him.

Why are you chasing me? the boy said.

Chasing you? the bear answered. I'm just trying not to burn.

3

I WOKE TO bad news in an email. A friend's death. Cause unknown. They found her in a hotel room. Her sister wrote me. I hadn't seen her for, what, 15 years?

I didn't make this story up, but it still counts. A story is a story.

Upstairs I could hear the neighbors' toddler, feet thumping across the floor like a herd of little deer. Mine, two years and nine months on this earth, sat beside me at the kitchen table, eating her oatmeal. Or not eating it, to be accurate, because it was still too hot. Blow, I told her. She blew. The steam rising like a ghost from her bowl fled before the quickness of her breath, and then returned. She was pregnant, she told me. Yeah? I said. Mmhmm, she said. With a monkey and a purple bear. They would come out of her belly in six days. Really? I said. Yes, she said. Why six? She wouldn't say.

4

A BOY DIES. He's young. A boy, like I said. Will all my stories be about death? Maybe. In any case, a soldier shot him. That is why the boy is dead. This is what soldiers do. They kill people. The soldier doesn't know, doesn't think, about the infinity of grief that will expand from such a simple movement of his index finger. Barely a twitch. He exerts more energy tying his boots. But how could he know? He's just a soldier and no more than a boy himself. And what does knowledge have to do with anything?

In any case, the boy who is dead walks and wanders. This is what the dead do. He never tires. He is always tired. He visits his mother and sits beside her on the bed, running his fingers through her hair. If only he could smell it. If he could, he knows it would smell of her shampoo, of cigarette smoke, of sadness. Her hand grips the covers tight. He places his own hand over hers and strokes her knuckles, her clenched fingers, but they do not let go. He visits his father. He is standing, smoking behind the house. The smoke rises. There is a lizard on the wall. The smoke makes it blink. Now his father is not standing anymore but crouching, shaking. The cigarette falls. He has never seen his father weep before, and he cannot bring himself to touch him. He visits his siblings. They are on the sofa, huddled close to watch a movie on their father's phone, and he kisses them, one by one, on the brow, a gesture he would not have permitted himself in life. He lies on his belly in the dirt of the yard and watches a solitary ant struggle to carry a blade of grass. He rolls onto his back and watches a pair of doves take flight from a lamppost. A cloud shaped like a rifle, no, a snake, drifts across the sky. The boy gets up and walks some more and finds his friends where they have gathered on the hillside, and he doesn't touch them, doesn't say a word. They are not playing, not arguing, not boasting or wrestling. He sits beside them, as silent as they are, scratching his neck where the bullet went in, tapping one knee with his fingers. If only they knew, he thinks, if only I could tell them that I am here.

5

I SAT BESIDE you and held your hand. For months, for years, I sat beside you. I'm going to die, you said. I know, I said, but not if you hold my hand. You smiled and closed your eyes again and squeezed my fingers and did not die for a little while longer. Finally you said, I want to die. I know, I said, and I lied to you and told you I would be okay. You squeezed my fingers and let yourself die. It took a while. Longer than a week. A year or two. Centuries. Just before you died, you opened your eyes to look at me. A tear fell from your eye. Just one tear. From your left eye. It tumbled down your cheek. And then you did die and I have not left you. I am here beside you, and I do not plan to let go of your hand.

6

NINA WAKES IN the night, inconsolable. Or really she doesn't wake, just cries, still in the grip of a nightmare. I rush in and pick her up and hold her until her eyes open, pacing her little bedroom, stroking and soothing her, kissing the tears from her cheeks. It's over now, I tell her, and I try to reassure her—because what does she know? How many times has she dreamed?—that the thing about dreams is that they end. You wake up and they're over. Gone. What I can't tell her and what won't leave my mind as I try to soothe her is that we will wake from this dream, too, the one in which I pace this dark room, holding her, her head heavy on my shoulder, my flesh and the tendons and muscles in my arms measuring the precise weight and softness of her, and I can't tell her how desperately I want this dream to never end.

7

IT HADN'T RAINED for weeks, and the leaves on the trees crisped up ahead of schedule, and my in-laws, who were visiting, complained that the sidewalks smelled of dog piss—they used a gentler word—that must have baked into the concrete where it splattered for lack of any downpour to wash it away. I hadn't noticed that, actually, but today it did rain, just a little bit, a mist that briefly licked the ground, a cruel tease for any thirsty plant but enough in the end to awaken the odors lying dormant in the dead, dry shells of things, and for a little while, ten minutes, if that, the city blossomed, alive and aglitter and stinking gloriously of piss.

8

TODAY IT WAS windy. Not just a breeze shaking the trees but proper heaving gusts, leaves flying everywhere, entire jagged branches scooting down the curb by the trash bins, potted shrubs knocked on their sides, and then it really began to blow: toddlers shrieking past in little rising vortices of clumped-up tissues and plastic bags and stuffed animals and greasy burger wraps, old ladies wheezing by in billowing backless hospital gowns, gasping for breath, hurling walkers and bedpans and curses, soiled sheets flapping like sails, bandages unraveling, snapping and frantic, catheters twisting like snakes, dark clouds of ash and ashtrays and cigarettes stubbed out after just one coughing drag, a sticky mist of spilled tequila and vermouth, bottle caps and little green plastic flossers like tiny stinging shields and swords, a swirling armada of hospital beds sailing past, a hail of pills, another gust, another, so much silent death sweeping blue and stale over everything and just me on this bench, sitting frozen, an anchor, a stone, a mountain, not an eyelash out of place.

9

THE SUN SETS over the sea. It is not a dramatic sunset, no baroque pinks and golds, just a gradual softening, then darkness. All the same, it is worth watching, reflected as it is in the infinite oily scales that sink and swell over the heaving skin of the sea. Oh, the colors! Did I say it wasn't dramatic? I lied. There are so many shades of blue and of gray and even white, especially where they meet up with yellow over there, with birds, with cloud, with wind. I am on a ferry. Did I mention that? On my way to meet a friend. The sun sets and children run and play on the deck and men drink and smoke, sitting with their legs crossed, and some of these birds are very far from shore. To the north and south and east, the water is a dismal gray. Everywhere but west, where it is glorious. One of the birds catches up with us, frantic, and lands for a moment on the deck. A thrush, I think, but what do I know? It doesn't rest. It flies away. What is it doing here, at sea? And what about me? I am going to meet a friend. The children stumble and their fathers pick them up, and one man leans to spit over the rail and another bends to kiss his infant daughter's tiny ear. He nibbles it and she grins, and the older kids skip and yowl and no one's looking anymore, not to the west anyway. No one notices that it's over. The sun is gone. It will be dark but it isn't yet. This happens every day.

10

AM I THE only one who feels—everywhere I go, on the subway, in the supermarket, on the bus, and on the sidewalk—like a bomb is about to go off here, an asteroid about to collide with the Earth? Like this, all of this, is the silent tracking shot at the beginning of a disaster film, the camera soaring by to scan the innocents, unwary, our obliviousness rendered poignant by the calamity that, in the very next shot, or the shot after that, is about to reveal its face?

11

A WOMAN GIVES birth to a rock. It is, as you might imagine, more than usually painful to give birth to a rock. She does not resent the rock for the pain it causes her because she has already carried it for the full forty weeks and she knows that the rock is hers, just as she, at this point, is the rock's. She tries to nurse it, but it will not nurse. She caresses it, but it will not coo. She tickles it, but it does not giggle. It does not cry, so she cannot soothe it. It does not piss or shit, so she cannot change its diapers. It is a rock. Does she love it? Have you understood nothing? She gave birth to it. It is hers, and she belongs to it. That is enough.

12

LAST NIGHT I dreamed about my mother for the first time since her death. She had written me an email, and I knew it was important to remember what it said, not the precise wording of the message itself necessarily but what it captured about her, her humor, the shape she took as she pushed her way through the world, the steadiness of her outrage, her stubbornness, her love for me. But of course I had forgotten it even before the dream had ended, and though she was there with me in the dream, she couldn't tell me what it said.

13

I AM TIRED. Is that a story?

How about this: Once upon a time I was not tired. Now I am.

14

NOTHING BAD HAPPENS in this story. Nothing sad. A bird flies. The air meets its wings. The sun rises. A man stands beside a window with his daughter in his arms. Outside an empty bus passes on an empty street. The sidewalks wet and gleaming. The sky still pink and gold. The few leaves that remain on the trees shiver with the wind. Together they are whispering.

What are they saying? Nina asks.

I don't know, I say. Listen.

15

IT WAS TIME to plant—past time, really—so I took Nina down to the community garden and showed her how. We pulled out what was left of the previous season's crops, all long past gone to seed, and we tilled the soil and tossed out all the rocks and weeds we found. There were shards of mussel shells, too, and bones from the compost heap. I left them there. Nina palmed a chicken bone, and I pretended not to notice. We mixed in some fresh compost from the bin, pushed the soil into long mounded rows, and with a stick poked holes into the valleys between them. In each hole we placed a seed. Rows of kale, rows of arugula, rows of radish, rows of chard. When we were done, we covered the seeds with soil and sprinkled them with water. If we keep coming back, I told her, and we give them enough water, something new will grow.

As we walked home, Nina produced the chicken bone. Can I eat it? she asked. No, I said, but if we plant it we can grow a chicken. I don't think she believed me.

Later, sitting beside me at the kitchen table, she helped me peel potatoes. Sticking out of one of them we found a worm. It had burrowed halfway through. It was a caterpillar, really, a gently variegated brown, more or less the same color as the potato in which it had resided. I told Nina to take it to her mother, but Livi didn't want anything to do with it, so we brought it out on the balcony and, at a loss, I flicked it down onto the street. Can you see it? she said. I could. Barely. It was squirming on the asphalt between parked motorcycles. What kind of moth, I wondered, would it have become? If things had worked out differently, that is, and it had been free to take the extraordinary trouble to weave a cocoon around itself and emerge as something else entirely? I meant to ask Nina, to see what she thought, but we both felt bad about the whole situation, so we went back inside and got to work on the carrots.

16

A HARD WIND blows against a cliff face. It can't go back. Wind is stubborn. It can't go down. The ground is in the way. It can't go through the cliff. So it goes up. It goes over. It moves on. The cliff remains the same. A little smaller perhaps. Perhaps diminished some.

17

IN THE KITCHEN I asked Nina what I should write a story about, and she said Chrysanthemum. She didn't mean the flower. She was talking about the mouse from the children's book, which is one of my favorites too. But that story has already been written and turned into a book, so I looked up chrysanthemums on my phone. They symbolize adversity, lamentation, death. Of course they do. I put the eggplant in the oven. Nina tried on her mother's shoes in front of the bedroom mirror. I made a salad: I washed the lettuce, shook it dry, diced a piece of onion, doused it with lemon juice and salt, and left it to mellow in a bowl. Adversity, lamentation, death! I sang aloud as I peeled a cucumber, slow and mournful: *Chrysanthemum, belly full of rum, I'll miss you forever, my chrysanthemum.* Adversity, lamentation, death! Nina was stumbling around, her mother's cowboy boots almost up to her hips, the earth tight with pain and joy and yearning. I sang to her. *Chrysanthemum, belly full of rum, I'll miss you forever, my chrysanthemum.*

No, Nina shouted. I want the story! She meant the one about the mouse.

18

LAST NIGHT WE had a Day of the Dead celebration at the garden. It was Eli's idea. This morning I walked down to retrieve my mother's photo from the altar. I got there at the same time as Montse, who still had traces of green face paint smeared around her eyes. She was there for the same reason that I was, and had brought a drill to take apart the altar. Her photo was a strange grainy blur, a photocopy of a blowup of a picture of a painting, a portrait of her mother as a young woman. I could make out the curve of a woman's cheek but not much more. In the original, she said, her mother was kissing her brother, but she had cut him out of the image. I didn't ask why. She asked me who mine was. My mother, I said. The photo was old, from sometime in the eighties, in Florida, Mom in a blond phase, standing in front of a bougainvillea in bloom, staring at the camera, her gaze soft. She looks beautiful, thoughtful, even happy. When did she die? Montse asked. Two months ago, I said. Was it, she paused, a bad death or? She didn't finish, as if the other kind had no name. It was bad, I told her. Her mother's was, too, she said, and though it had been sixty years ago, when Montse was just fourteen, she wanted to tell me about it, urgently. She had cancer, in her kidneys, Montse said. They gave her morphine, but in those days they couldn't do much. They can't do much now, I said. Montse told me about a woman she knew, the wife of a friend. She was pregnant, four months in, and when she went in for a routine ultrasound they found cancer everywhere. They weren't looking for it, but they found it: not new life but certain death. They told her she should abort the pregnancy, that her cancer was so advanced the baby wouldn't make it anyway. If she began treatment immediately she might live two years, but no more than that for sure. Imagine, Montse said. What would you do? Go on a trip around the world? She ended the pregnancy and started chemo, and a few months later, miraculously, the doctors, the same ones who told her she only had two years, said the tumor had shrunk far more than they'd expected, that she would live, she would be okay. Imagine, Montse said, being told that you were going to die, that it was all over, and then suddenly . . . She didn't finish the sentence. As if it were life that was unnamable. I told Montse that my mother had stopped eating and died a week later. Why did she stop? Montse asked. Because she didn't want to live like that, I told her. Montse asked me, You're not in a hurry, are you? We took the pan de muerto from the altar. The dead had already had their chance with it. Montse found a knife and a clean plate and sliced the bread in even chunks while I washed a few glasses in cold water from the spigot on the wall beneath the shelter we had built the summer before. Adrianna and Eli showed up, and the four of us sat around the wobbly wooden table in the sun and ate the sugary bread together, dipping it in the coffee that Montse poured from a thermos. It left my fingers sticky. Eli told me she had hidden the bottle I had brought for the altar so that no one would see it through the fence and be tempted to break in. She laughed and said, I didn't want you to think the muertos drank it all. I got up and washed my hands in the spigot and dried them with a handkerchief and said my goodbyes before I picked up the photo of my mother, so pretty in the Florida sun.

19

WALKING DOWN THE street to the garden, I explained to Nina that we had to water the seeds every day to make them grow. But why? she asked. If we didn't take care of them, I told her, they would die. Like Grandma died? she asked.

Yeah, I said. Like Grandma.

And if we had taken care of Grandma, she asked, would she still have died?

I took my time unlocking the padlock and unwinding the chain on the gate to the garden. I pulled the gate open and let it swing shut behind us. No, I said. We took good care of Grandma, but she was old and she died anyway.

And if we take care of her now, Nina asked, will she be alive?

I gathered three of the big gray watering cans and another smaller green one, and carried them all over to the spigot by the wall. I filled the gray ones and closed the tap when just an inch of water had filled the little green one so that Nina would be able to lift it. Grandma is dead, I told her, and handed her the watering can, but we can take care of her now by remembering her, by loving her. Love is how you make things live, I said. It's the only way. The cans were heavy and spilled a little as I lugged them down to the planters and emptied them one by one over the long rows I had dug, tiny green leaves budding forth already every few inches from the soil.

Look, I said, the seeds have sprouted. But Nina wasn't listening. She was pulling chicken bones from the compost. Bones! she shouted. I want more bones!

20

CAN A QUESTION be a story?

Maybe that's the wrong question to ask. Or the wrong way to ask it.

Narrative, in the best of circumstances, is mildly obscene. It plucks a few elements from the whirlwind of god's howling grace, holds them still long enough to shove them into a sort of gated corral called a story. Most things it leaves out. Like that caterpillar flicked from the balcony and left to writhe on the asphalt. Where does that fit in your butterfly fantasy? And what about the things that are not things anymore? What if the gate swings open and all the fence posts fall down? If things have, shall we say, *broken*, can a story be anything other than a question?

21

WHAT IF BENEATH the soil there isn't just soil and more soil, then rocks and slurry, then steaming fissures all the way down to bubbling molten core? What if, instead, the ground beneath us is a shallow crust and barely there, like the surface of a pond in early winter, and below that just cold, dark water flowing until the very end of space, the sloshing substance of the universe with only this thin, fragile skin between our shoes and it? And if in that frigid substrate anything can live, perhaps some variety of fish can, white and soft, mooning around in the all-encompassing darkness, eyeless perhaps, unpigmented. And if anything can be communicated between those fish, if they are fish, and us here above in this brittle world, then what? What words would they whisper if they could whisper words at all? What do they know that we don't? What do they understand about love?

22

SHALL I TRY to answer? They are not fish, really. They have no scales or eyes, and they are mouthless, gill-less, without fins or limbs of any kind. They are vagrant oblong lozenges of light glimpsed as if in a dream through the blur of grief. Are they even down there? I take it on faith that they are, that it's not just emptiness forever. What are they saying? Listen. The dead are not talking about love. They have no news to impart, no messages. They want your fingers, your fingernails, the tickling loose thread in the neckband of your shirt. They want to know what it is to grip a pencil in your teeth, to pluck a hair, to shit. They want to feel the caress of someone's eyelash on your cheek. They want to be bitten and to bite. They want dry throat in the morning, shivers, fever, backache, broken toe. They want tongue. They want to swallow something hot. They want to scrape hard against the rocks.

23

ON MONDAY THERE was a full lunar eclipse. The earth got in the way of the moon. On Tuesday Livi called me with a complicated request: our apartment building is number sixty-four and we had received a package meant for building number six, apartment four, a few blocks down the hill on the same street. She was expecting a package from the same sender but it hadn't arrived. If we had theirs, perhaps they had ours down in number six.

On my way home I stopped and rang the bell. A young woman answered. I tried to explain through the intercom but only managed to confuse her. She buzzed me up anyway. I climbed the stairs and found her waiting outside her door. The door to the apartment next to hers opened too. An old woman stuck her head out and stood in the doorway beside a large orange cat. The cat tried to slip through the old woman's legs but she blocked it with her feet. I smiled. She did not smile back. I explained the situation to the young woman, who said she didn't have our package but that she would come up to get hers. The cat tried again to get out. The young woman scowled at the old woman, who scowled back. I left and walked up the hill, the sun setting behind it, toward home. Our package never showed.

Today a man knocked at the door. He had a package, he said. Olivia? he said. Yes, I said. He had me sign for it and rushed back to his van. I read the side of the box. It said, Auto Parts Store. We don't own a car. I texted Livi, You got a package from an auto parts store. She texted back that she had not ordered any auto parts. I looked at the shipping label. Olivier, it said. I laughed. I tried to call the phone number on the return label, but it was a missing a digit. The box is still sitting on the table.

In any case, we couldn't see the eclipse. Where we live, the moon wasn't up in time. We would have had to have been on the other side of the planet, an ocean away. Which is to say that the earth got in the way of our view of the earth getting in the way of the moon. Later, though, I saw it rise and hang huge and orange over the city to the east. I had to run to catch the bus, but I made it just in time and I found a seat facing backward so that I could watch it through the window until, after just a block, the city got in the way.

24

I KEEP LISTENING to the same song again and again. Duke Ellington playing "Single Petal of a Rose." It's barely a song, just him alone on piano. No horns, no sweeping orchestral anything. Later a bass comes in and joins him, but by then it feels like a dream. His left hand plays the same open phrase over and over, four rising notes. More of a question than a phrase. His right hand isn't idle, but it's mainly commenting on what the left one is doing: winking, shrugging, echoing, reassuring. You keep thinking that the phrase will find a way to close and fold into a melody, that it will become something else, a song with recognizable structures, but it doesn't. At first it's gentle, wistful, patient and then increasingly mournful and insistent. More than once the song seems like it's going to end, but then it comes back hungry, furious, with each repetition more anguished and alone. And then calm again, soft, somehow freer. When the song ends he's still playing that same phrase, but it and perhaps he have been transformed. The question has not been answered, but that doesn't matter anymore. It has been asked.

25

I WAS GOING to write a story about a tiger stalking through a forest at night. "A tiger stalks through a forest," it was going to begin. "Night had fallen," it would go on, "but the jungle was alive with scent." The tiger was going to smell traces left by all the animals it hoped to catch and eat, its nose mapping the terrain in four dimensions: over there a monkey that had leapt from tree trunk to tree trunk fifteen minutes before the tiger passed, here a small deer that had been nibbling at the underbrush twenty minutes earlier, there a farmer who had hurried down the path to the village, jogging to get home to his family before sunset, when the tigers come out. But the trails would all lead to naught. The tiger would encounter no prey—no monkey, no deer, no farmer. Not even a mouse. It would stalk and stalk but find nothing. Its magnificent strength would go wasted, the perfection of its violence unrealized. The tiger would wander a landscape of ghosts, its hunger growing as the scents grew ever fainter, the world itself losing clarity, fading into the uniformity of want.

I hadn't figured out how the story would end—because it couldn't just end like that—and I was thinking it over as I walked through the city, the air alive with that lunatic autumn clarity, even the dull doorways sparkling. While I was waiting to cross the street, I noticed a man sitting on the sidewalk outside a building that had once been a bank. He looked about my age but worse for wear, nearly bald, his skin gray, his clothes oily and torn. I had seen him sitting there before. Beside him lay a hat containing a few coins that passersby had tossed him, and beside the hat was a tiger. Not the tiger from my story but a plush one, matted now, small and fat, its limbs like sausages sewn into blue jeans and a football jersey as faded as its fur. It sat there grinning dumbly at the ankles of the people walking by. One of its eyes was missing. The black thread that formed its mouth hung loose. I dug around in my jeans, but my pockets were empty and the light changed, so I crossed the street and went back to wondering how to end this story.

26

IN THE GARDEN we were moving old rotten boards and scrap wood from one place to another. Just to get them out of the way. Later, we knew, we would have to move them again, and for the same reason. It was only when we reached the bottom of the pile that things began to get interesting. Worms wriggled everywhere. Cesca lifted a sliver of a board and found a millipede. How it squirmed! Imagine how good you'd be at squirming if you had one thousand legs. Or no legs. I picked up a plank and found a lizard. It was squirming, too, panicking, its home torn apart by giants, by monsters, nothing to protect it from the dangers of the sky. I walked it over to our new woodpile, and found it a dark and sheltered corner. It scurried off and disappeared. On the other side of the garden, in the raised beds we built last year, the seeds that Nina and I had planted and watered every morning were already sprouting. Maybe this isn't much of a story. Nothing dramatic happened. Not from this perspective, anyway. But think of the stories the millipede could tell, and the lizard, and the sprouts. The drama!

27

HERE AT THE top of the world, I see many things. I see vines and creeping tendrils, and delicate purple flowers lit from below by the sun so that their petals glow as if aflame at the edges. I see birds with translucent wings in great flocks and murmurations, like the mobs of starlings we used to see curling over great suburban parking lots, only these birds are beneath me, not above, and they do not darken the sky but only cause the light to flicker almost imperceptibly as if the density of the air were shifting as they gather and disperse. There is no pollution up here. Nothing decays. I don't know how I ended up here. I have no memory of the ascent. I haven't met anyone else here, but I haven't really looked. I suppose I would have seen someone coming. Because let me tell you, the view is something else. I can see the mountaintops, of course, and the mountainsides falling away beneath them, and the highest points of the tallest buildings and the highest trees. I can see all the rooftops, bristling with antennas and satellite dishes. I can just make out the tops of everyone's heads, and by everyone, I mean every last creature. Even the ones that, properly speaking, do not have heads. Bivalves and whatnot. Unless they're hiding in the mud. I can see down into all the crevices carved by water or wind or human hands or explosives or machines, into the wells and the mines and the open graves. I can see into the oceans and the rivers and the puddles. When the light is right, in flashes I can see into their depths, too, the shipwrecks and blind unpigmented fish there, the swollen cadavers and the crabs racing to conceal themselves beneath the sand. I can see the sorrow that blows through it all like wind and the grinding thirst and yearning that join everything together like threads of a cloth being woven on the run. When the humidity allows, I can see the love of everything for everything like a secret pattern, the weave within the weave. But today, like most days, the clouds are thick, and though I know what's there beneath me, or I tell myself that I do, I can't see anything, none of it, not even the buttons on my shirt, my knees, my own stupid feet.

28

I WOKE UP before anyone else and slipped out of bed in silence. I made coffee and worked for half an hour before waking Nina. As she does every night, she had crept into our bed around midnight. I gave her shoulder a gentle squeeze. She sat up in the dark, alarmed. I can't see! she shouted. It's just your hair, Livi said. Your hair is in your eyes. But for a moment we really were afraid.

29

AGAIN, IT WAS supposed to rain, but it did not rain, again.

30

I LAY ON the empty beach, the warm sun an orange glow behind my eyelids. I listened to the sound of the waves breaking to my left and then my right, a hidden sandbar splitting the surf in stereo, roaring, growling, hissing, sighing, first here, then there, then here again. And if I stilled my thoughts and did my best to synchronize my breathing to the rhythm of the waves, I felt a rising certainty that I was about to learn something important, something vital and final, even, that if I just listened close enough, the waves were going to reveal it in their whispering. Then as if from a great distance, I heard Nina's tiny voice calling to me. I opened my eyes and saw her standing naked beside her mother, shivering with glee. She was singing happy birthday to her toes, which had, until a moment earlier, been concealed beneath the sand.

31

SOMETIMES I TRIED to imagine the world without you. To prepare myself because it was so obviously coming. Sometimes I even wished for it, to spare you the many indignities. But my imagination was poor. It was like a crude photo-editing tool: this same scene, this room, just one less person in it. You would be gone, but the cushions and the wall behind where you had been sitting on the sofa would be filled in with the appropriate colors and textures. So would the books stacked haphazard on the shelf, the glass-topped coffee table with your notebooks and red and black pens and piled scrap paper and the rings of condensation where your water glass had been. The one I kept filling, nagging you. Drink, Mama. I imagined an emptiness replacing you, but the essential continuity would go unbroken. It would be seamless, as if you had simply vanished or never been there at all. I did not understand that without you the room would be gone, the wall and the books and the shelf and the table. The apartment and the whole building would be gone, and the air inside them, and me, too, or whatever I was then that I am not anymore.

32

MARIAM WROTE TO me. Fuck the poetics, she wrote. How you holding up?

33

NINA DID NOT want to leave the playground, but all the other kids were going, too, so she didn't argue for long. We walked a block in the direction of the hospital where she was born and had just turned toward home when I saw an old woman stepping out of a building ahead of us. She was pushing a baby carriage and pulling, unmistakably, a pig on a leash. It was not a large pig, but it was not small. It was a medium pig. There was no baby in the baby carriage, it turned out, just an elderly Chihuahua. Look! I said to Nina. A pig on a leash! She was not impressed. Why shouldn't anyone walk a pig on a leash while pushing a miniature decrepit dog in a stroller? The pig was sniffing at the sidewalk with great enthusiasm, as if on the trail of something unimaginably desirable. Perhaps it was just hungry. The old woman had her own plans. She tugged hard at the leash, yanking the pig's front trotters off the cement. The pig was outraged. It wheezed and whined in panic and fury, its snout swinging wildly over the concrete. The old woman whacked it on the flanks with a rolled and taped-up newspaper and, with surprising strength, dragged the pig away down the sidewalk. The Chihuahua looked on from its perch in the carriage, unmoved. Why, Nina asked, is the pig so angry?

34

NINA'S TURN:

There were two hoopoes. There were three hoopoes. There were four hoopoes. There were so many hoopoes! Then a crocodile came and it bit the hoopoes. What happened? A dragonfly came. There were no more hoopoes and the dragonfly said, What happened? We don't know. We don't know what happened. Then a lion came and it ate the dragonfly. Then a frog came and it said, What happened? We don't know. A snake came and it ate the frog. What happened? We don't know.

35

I SPENT THE morning alone in the garden, watering, tidying, pulling weeds. I will admit, to you at least, that I don't always know if the plants I am uprooting are what we call weeds or something that someone else planted purposefully and that might, if I had left them for a few more weeks, have turned into something magnificent.

36

MAYBE THERE IS a hole in the wind. A quiet room, some calm and secret cave, a place to rest without retreating. Last night the wind howled hard. All night. It was still blowing when I woke. I held Nina in one arm and with the other opened the blinds in the living room, in her bedroom, the kitchen. Our morning ritual while her mother sleeps. Look, I said. Look at the wind. Look how the trees are dancing. She looked. I asked the questions that I ask each morning. How did you sleep? I said. Fine, she said. As she always does, her voice still fogged with sleep. Did you have dreams? I asked. Sometimes she says no. Sometimes she remembers them and tells me. Often she makes one up. I can always tell. This time she didn't. I don't know, she said. You don't remember? I asked. No, she said. I told her that I didn't remember mine either, though I did, a little bit.

With my right arm, I made the morning's oatmeal. I held her in my left. I pulled the pot from the drainboard and placed it on the burner. I poured in a cup or two of oatmeal, however much milk. I turned on the flame. Do you want raisins? I asked. Surprise: she did. I added raisins. I added cinnamon. Do you want to smell the cinnamon? I asked. Her tiny nose craned forward and sniffed at the jar. When it was ready, I spooned the oatmeal into her bowl, cooled it with milk from the fridge, dug a spoon from the silverware drawer, and left it beside the bowl on the table. The wind had not let up. Vortices of brown and yellow leaves were skipping around the street below us.

Do you want me to put you in your chair? I asked. Or hug a little longer? Hug, she answered as she always does, and tightened her grip around my shoulders. I only ask because I want to hear her say it. Are you ready? I asked. She shook her head. Not yet, she said.

I do not mean to suggest that Nina or her fleeting hugs are a secret cave, a home, a hole in the wind. She is a little girl, her own person, too vast to be reduced to such a role. I am wondering, though, if this story I am telling, these words, could be just such a hole. Sometimes. For a little while. Now.

37

WALKING UP THE hill I met a bird. A magpie with long and enviably gleaming blue-black tail feathers. The hill was steep, and I was panting from the effort. The magpie hopped from rock to rock in front of me, its long tail bobbing with each jump. It turned to me. Fly, stupid man, it said. Why do you walk when you could fly? I can't fly, I told the magpie. Look at me, I said. I'm not like you. I don't have wings or feathers. Stupid man, the magpie said again, and flew away.

38

THE FLIGHT WAS late so I missed the flight. I missed the flight so I was late. It's late. I miss you. On the flight, all was mist out the window, lazy cartoon limbo, cloud and white, then more cloud, more white, more mist, and finally light, yellow and then blue. The color of airport, the color of city, of humankind, the living, whatever this is supposed to be. It doesn't matter now. I missed the flight. In the airport I asked where I should go, and they told me go through those doors and up the escalator to the gate, and I walked and walked but I couldn't find the doors, or not those doors, just some doors. I went through them and up the escalator, but there was no gate, just more doors and escalators and wide halls with polished floors. And I thought of you in airports, always in airports for so many years, hating airports, of all the times you called me while you waited at the gate, voices echoing behind you. And I, in an airport of my own, waited at my gate with echoing voices of my own and all the screens with the gates and the times and so much news and sports, but this time I couldn't find the gate, only more wide halls and endless duty-free and escalators leading to the duty-free. There weren't even any doors. I waited anxiously and passed through immigration twice, and they stamped my passport and kept stamping until there were no empty pages left and it was no longer clear if I was coming or going or what country I was in, if there was a country anymore. I found the doors. I found the baggage claim. I found my bag. I was outside. It was cold. How would I get back in? I stood outside the airport in the cold. I couldn't call you. I couldn't tell you that I missed the flight, that I would be late, that the flight was late, that I miss you and it hurts.

39

FROM THE AIR I could see a city, a wind farm, clouds. Little snakes of vapor dancing at the tip of the wing. After a while I couldn't see earth or sea or anything, just this rough skin of cloud, but I knew what was beneath it. I had an idea, anyway. And I knew that you were neither below the cloud-skin nor with me here above it, that you weren't anywhere, though I could still say your name and speak of you, and my words, I must believe, still carry meaning. Because a sign without a referent is a dead thing. Is a nothing is a nil. Is a spirit, perhaps. Is a haunt. And I thought, up there above the clouds, of a day not long ago when I was walking through the park and, finding myself sufficiently alone in a sufficiently secluded zone, I tried to speak to you. You didn't answer, of course, or not in words that anyone could hear, but when a flurry of little birds stormed above the path ahead, I understood their presence to be your voice, your words, signs without referents from a sign without a referent. They didn't mean anything. Nothing, anyway, other than: See this. Or: Look here. Or maybe: Come. Sit. This is a good place to sit. So I sat and watched the birds and spoke to you. Knowing how annoyed you'd be by all of this. And here, wherever this is, still I try to listen. To see and to look. Even if it is only at these silent clouds, pinkening now and darkening, which you, too, would have liked. And now at the darkness, where the clouds no longer are.

40

WE DROVE UP into the mountains. There was snow. There were trees. Redwoods or firs. There was endless dome of sky. All the birds were crows, except the ravens. The moon hummed above us, half full. Later the sun sank over the lake, beaming at a coy diagonal from behind the clouds like in some cheap stage-set heaven. We saw a lenticular cloud hanging low above the water like a lone pink flying saucer, and a sticker on the bumper of a blue pickup truck that expressed such a virulent racism, genocidal fantasy so whimsically voiced, that I could not breathe for a good long minute after reading it.

41

IT SNOWED AND snowed and the snow silenced everything.

42

SHE DIDN'T OFFER, and I knew better than to ask her for the whole story, but her brother may be losing it. Or has already lost it. Whatever it is or was or may yet be, he can't find it. He's been sending hundreds of texts of garbled nonsense to the youngest niece. Just letters, not even words. So many letters. A sign without a referent is a dead thing. Accustomed to adults behaving incomprehensibly, she humors him. But clearly he is not doing well. He's gotten worse, his sister says. Is that a story, waiting for bad news? Traffic lights, blinking turn signals, pitted tire shop parking lots, railroad ties, overgrown barbed wire hidden in the vines what is that strange and horrible smell. This is the end of the line. That's not a metaphor; we could see it right there in front of us: a log laid across the tracks, then a fence a few yards farther down. More barbed wire. The sky a brief and garish pink. On the other side of the mountains, desert.

43

WITHOUT A SOUND, snow falls from the trees onto the snow. Oh god, there was a world here once.

44

I WALKED IN the woods. Snow was falling in wet and heavy flakes. An owl swooped down and landed on my shoulder. Owl, I said. Correct, said the owl. What is it? I said. Crow, said the owl. Watch out for crow. I thanked the owl, and the owl flew off. I kept walking. With each step my boots disappeared into the snow. It was blowing sideways now and so hard that I left no tracks. I could only see a tree or two ahead. Beyond that just whiteness and blur. A crow fluttered down and landed on my shoulder. Crow, I said. Correct, said the crow. What do you want? I said. Bear, said the crow. Watch out for bear. I thanked the crow, and the crow flew off. It was all I could do to lift my boots and take another step. The air was swirling white. Where was I going? I felt a weight on my shoulder. I looked and saw thick brown fur. A paw. It was enormous. It was a bear's. Bear, I said. Correct, said the bear. It's winter, I said. Bears sleep in winter. Shouldn't you be sleeping?

Sleep, said the bear. Watch out for sleep. I thanked the bear. But how will I know? I asked. How will I know if I am sleeping? The bear didn't answer. It loped off and disappeared into the snow. It was nearly dark. I could barely see my hands. In the silence of the snow I heard a crow caw. I knew I should be cold but I wasn't. I heard an owl hoot and hoot again. It occurred to me that I should be scared, that I might freeze, but more than anything I was puzzled. How will I know if I am sleeping? I kept walking, the snow and the darkness erasing everything around me, everything but this.

45

I DROVE DOWN the mountain, through the blinding snow. I did not slip or skid or crash. I did not get us stuck in the storm. I did not die this time. Again I did not die. We made it to the valley, beneath the snow line. The sky cleared. The roads cleared. Hail hammered the car.

46

THE TV WAS on all day every day, and all week there were rats in every show and every movie that we watched. Cartoon rats and CGI rats, mutant rats and alien rats and people who mysteriously transformed into human-shaped statues composed entirely of rats, which swiftly disintegrated as the rats disentangled themselves, wriggling and climbing over each other to escape this inelegant unasked-for collectivity. The undergrowth crawled with rats. Trash cans jumped, and rats climbed and scurried out of them. There were rotting corpses with rotting gums and grinning rats that popped comically out of rotting zombie corpses' mouths. Rats emerged from people's bellies, whiskers atwitch, sniffing. Surprise! Is this what death is, a rat? A heap of rats? Rot and gore and violent haunting? Terror? You know how I'm going to answer. You can guess, at least. No. Death is not a rat. Not a live one, anyway.

47

I WAS ON a plane all day, or perhaps for several days, sleeping a poorly drugged sleep stretched across the seats, then wandering through airports like a ghost. I washed my face in a restaurant bathroom, nearly fell asleep on the bus on the way to pick up Nina. We sat on a park bench. She ate a tangerine and half of a banana. I hugged her tight and told her I that loved her. I love you, too, she said. I love you more, I said. I love you more, she said. We could have kept going but let it go at that.

48

AFTER INSISTING THAT she was not tired and didn't want to go to sleep or even hear a story, Nina curled herself into my arms and asked me to tell her a story. The one about the time I met a tiny monkey. I have never met a tiny monkey and have never implied otherwise. But I told her nonetheless that one day I was walking down the road with my dog, Chuleta. She died a year and a half ago. She had been living with my ex at the time, and I hadn't seen her for more than a year before that. I didn't tell Nina any of this. I didn't tell her anything for a while because I had fallen asleep. Her voice woke me up. *Tell the story!* she said. I told her there were tall trees all along both sides of the road. I didn't know where the story was going, but I figured I could improvise and that a tiny monkey might appear in the trees when the moment was right. Before I could get another sentence out, I fell asleep again. Nina woke me again. *Tell the story!* she said. We had a shopping cart, I said. We were pushing it. Again I fell asleep. I don't know for how long. *Tell the story!* We were filling it with leaves, I said. I didn't know why. Leaves? I was more than half unconscious even as I spoke—my words at this point were issuing directly from sleep—but it didn't matter anymore how and when or even if the tiny monkey would appear, because Nina was sleeping too.

49

SITTING BESIDE ME on the couch, Nina noticed the constellation of tiny holes at the bottom my shirt. They appear in all my tee shirts eventually. I don't know what causes them, but since I haven't smoked for years and can't blame falling embers, I blame my belt buckle, though maybe it's my zipper. Nina was puzzled too. What are these little holes? she said. Before I could answer, she asked, Why don't you cut them out? That would make a bigger hole, I said. Then you cut it out, she said. But then, I said, there'd be a bigger hole. Then you cut it out, she said, delighted by the direction this was going in. But then, I said, there would be nothing left but hole. She grinned, her eyes glowing at the thought.

50

AT THE PLANETARIUM we learned that Jupiter's red spot is actually a hurricane twice the size of the planet Earth and that its size is not constant—it was once three times as big as Earth—but its violence is. We learned that for all its apparent enormity, the sun is small compared to many stars, and that even galaxies are like grains of sand or motes of dust, something tiny, anyway, something insignificant. The man who delivered this lecture on infinity impressed me mainly with his small-mindedness, but maybe I am being arrogant and overly harsh and took it too personally when he suggested, on seeing us walk in, that Nina was too young to understand the secrets of the universe that he intended to impart. In any case, he thought it important to insist that among this vast multiplicity of worlds it is a certainty that what he called intelligent life must exist elsewhere, too, which seemed to me beside the point.

Why bother contemplating immensity if all you hope to encounter is some version of yourself?

It was a tiny planetarium, hardly meriting the name, really, just an unheated room with a few folding chairs lined up around an old projector beaming blurry images of the heavens onto an inverted dome suspended from the ceiling. In a corner stood a foam or maybe plastic model of the sun to which a smaller blue sphere representing the Earth was attached via a short mechanical arm. Nina ran over and kneeled before it, wrapping her arms around the ball of the sun. Not in worship but in something more immediate: love. I grinned, proud of her, and she hugged it hard until the man who had given the lecture came over and snarled something about how difficult those things are to replace.

51

CAN AN IMAGE be a story? I don't mean one that suggests the possibility of other, more exciting events taking place outside the frozen timeline of the frame, like a pietà, or a newspaper photo of a cop with his knee on someone's back, or a film still of action hero, hard-eyed, finger on the trigger. I mean a fragment that points to nothing else. If such a thing can be imagined.

52

FINALLY IT RAINED. Brake lights smeared the streets with red.

53

I LOOKED OUT the window of the bus at the cars blurring past and the people bobbing by with their umbrellas and their necks and chins and nostrils, and at all the impossible colors of the fruit stacked outside the greengrocers, papaya, pomegranate, tomato, lemon, tangerine, and I thought, why is that not a story? Not the fruit but this fullness? The nonstop drama of being overflowing its borders? But it isn't, is it? This is just this. It doesn't count.

54

I WENT TO the dentist and demanded that he pull out all my teeth. Insurance will never cover it, he said. That's okay, I said, because I don't have insurance. Well, then, he said, and licked his lips. Eight hundred dollars a tooth. I looked in my wallet. I had forty bucks. Payment plans available, the dentist said with a grin, but I knew my credit was shot. You're a tooth-puller, I said. Have you no pride? These teeth should be anywhere but here! I was shouting. The dentist had the hygienists escort me to the curb. Who, I yelled at the passing cars, who will pull these dreadful bones from my gums? Who will relieve me of this mouth full of death? The police came, and I cursed them, too, until finally I got my wish, just like that, every last tooth, awful, awful things.

55

LITTLE DEAD MAMA, can I put you in my pocket? Can I hold you on my forearm like I did Nina when she was new? Or here in my empty palm? Can I prop you on my shoulder like a cartoon angel-devil? We could laugh at the same things we always did, only you would be smaller and visible only to me. Can I bring you everywhere like a lucky marble or a string of worry beads? If I do, will you stick around this time? Because I don't know what I would do if I dropped you, if I lost you on the bus, if a pickpocket made away with you or some awful bird swooped down and carried you off for a snack. What would I have then? What diminishment of this diminishment would be left, what shade, what breeze of what used to be you? Is that how this will go? Will you just keep getting smaller? Little dead mama, how can I keep what little of you remains?

56

WITH THE BONES in my gums and the bones in my head and the bones that vault my lungs and my heart and the bones that stiffen my fingers and legs, with these and other bones I will find you a place, a palace, a home.

Can a promise be a story? Perhaps, but only an unfinished one.

57

IN THE END it rained for days. I did my best to stay inside. I put on my slippers, turned up the heat, made a cup of tea, and sat in the armchair by the balcony, reading a novel. A magpie landed on the balcony railing just outside the window. The glass was cloudy with condensation, but I was pretty sure it was the same bird that had spoken to me a few days earlier, before the rains, and sure enough, it knocked with its beak against the glass. Hello, I said. You again. It must be awfully cold out there. And wet. The magpie knocked once more. I mean, flying is cool, but it must be awful to have to nest outdoors when the weather is so bad, I said. The magpie didn't speak. It just kept pecking at the glass with its beak. I'd let you into this nice, dry room, I said, but I suppose your feathers keep you warm enough and your wings could always fly you somewhere warmer. The magpie's beak broke through the glass. Hey! I said, but the magpie kept pecking and widening the hole, calmly, systematically, until the entire pane slid in shards from its frame and crashed to the floor at my feet. A cold wind blew rain onto my neck. Stupid man, said the magpie. Fly, stupid man, fly! Then off it flew, and I heard only the dark flutter of its wings.

58

THIS MORNING, AS I hurried to get dressed, Nina danced around the apartment singing, *Ay-ay-ay, I am alive.* A little later, walking to the office, the sun flared bright and low off the roofs and windows of the cars, blinding me with the glare. Way off in the distance, in the spaces between the buildings, I could see it reflecting off the sea. I would turn a corner and lose it for a block, then round a bend, and there it would be again, a spike in the eyes, obliterating color and form, softening everything. I knew it wouldn't last and that I would forget it like I forget everything, so I tried to take pictures to capture it, but later, when I sat down and looked at my phone, I found that the photos I had taken were just white—pure, empty light.

59

WALKING THROUGH THE park on my way to the office, I heard a terrible sound coming from the hillside above me. Snarling, then snapping and awful low rattling groans. It didn't sound like a dog. I couldn't help myself. I was curious. I stepped off the path and climbed up. Others, I saw, had walked this way before: a trail of bare and hardened dirt led up between the bushes. The sounds got louder as I climbed. At the top of the hill the path opened to the edge of a playground. I recognized it. I had been there with Nina, but it wasn't one of her favorites. It was ramshackle and desolate, the benches missing slats, the seesaw rusting, one of the swings torn and dragging in the dirt. And there it was, in the corner by the basketball court. It was a monster, of course. I feel bad using that word—such a slur—but that's what she was. She had the form of a woman, bent and hardened, with four arms and wild hair. Her eyes were gray and cloudy, her mouth smeared with blood and feathers. She had what looked like half a pigeon in one hand. She froze when she saw me and clutched the ruins of the bird to her breast, as if I might want to snatch it from her.

I have some experience with monsters, and I knew the best thing to do was stay calm. I took a seat on the nearest bench and crossed my legs. The monster reared and hissed. Are you okay? I asked. She answered with a ferocious growl and tossed the rest of the pigeon into her mouth. For a moment, a twitching three-toed foot protruded from her lips. It seemed to wave at me. You don't have to be okay, I said. I mean, I'm not okay, really. So if you're not, you're not alone. The monster crouched, then burst forward, charging me, all four of her arms tearing at the air at once as if she were grabbing at invisible strands and pulling herself forward. I knew she wouldn't do anything. She stopped just shy of my knee, snapped her teeth inches from my nose, then sat on her haunches in the dirt. Her feet were twisted, her curling toenails long and yellow. She smelled of peppermint. I thought a song might help. I looked away, up at the trees, and did my best to make it seem that I was singing to myself, for my own amusement. I started with "Moon River," but that seemed to agitate her, so I switched to "Old Man River," which, to my surprise, did the trick. I'm not much of a singer, but by the third verse she was swaying and even grunting in time to the refrain, *He just keeps rollin', he just keeps rollin' along*. I was late for work, but when I reached the end of the song, I didn't want to stop, so I started from the beginning again, and when I was a few verses into it, I looked down and saw that one of the monster's hands was in mine. She squeezed it and stroked my palm. You'll be okay, she whispered, and in that moment, at least, I believed her.

60

IT'S THE HOLIDAY, so I made applesauce and latkes, and Nina helped me peel the apples and potatoes, or at least she sat on the counter beside me while I peeled them and sniffed the cinnamon before I shook it into the saucepan. We had gone to the market that morning to buy a Christmas duck, but it turned out that there were no ducks because influenza is killing them all. It's very difficult right now for the ducks, the woman behind the poultry counter told me, her brow furrowed in distress. Then she returned to her cleaver and shears, dismembering chickens for other people's pots. We bought lamb instead and went home and cooked the latkes and ate and rested and went out again to see a band play in a square downtown. I've already forgotten their name, but they were filled with youth and energy and their music reminded me of a brass band I had seen approximately a thousand years ago at a warehouse party in Oakland at which I got epically drunk on bourbon and Vicodin and malt liquor and plum brandy that a friend had brought back from Romania. For a while, if memory serves, I was dancing at the head of the band as we marched around the party and out into the street. Could that be? Probably not. My stomach churns to think of it, but I had fun that night. High above the square, seagulls circled. Look, Nina said, the birds are dancing. The sky went pink, and Livi pointed at what at first looked like birds but turned out to be a great burst of bats all taking flight at once from a rooftop and dispersing in silence as the night unspooled violet around us.

61

YESTERDAY, OR MAYBE the day before, my sister texted me a photo of the yard beside her house. The bay had risen almost to her porch, and it wasn't even raining. A king tide, they're called. I remembered a time when I was there alone with my mother for a long weekend and the bay rose even higher, flooding most of the lawn. It hadn't rained then either. The water just kept rising. That was eight years ago. My mother could walk well enough then, and she wandered around outside alone, staring at the water all around her. I stayed indoors and took photos through the big bay window. I still have them on my phone. You can see that the tide had covered the roots of the myrtle tree and made it almost to the base of the old oak in the middle of the lawn. The hammock floated inches above the surface. The photos are blurry. I guess the light was low, and I must have been a dozen yards away and had to zoom. So Mom stands as if in a mist, looking so small and so lost and yet so determined to see what was coming. I was a little worried it would wash her away. It did, of course, only not in the way I had feared. I thought of sending my sister the photo, but I knew it would make her sadder, so I didn't send a photo at all, just texted and asked what she was planning to cook for Christmas dinner.

62

THE TRAINS WERE delayed and the platform was full, and when it came, the train was full, too, but the beach, when we got off, was empty. Nina wanted to be naked, and even though it was Christmas Day, it was warm enough, so we helped her take off her clothes, and she rolled in ecstasy in the cool sand. The waves crashed in like they do. The sun sank, as it does. The sky was cloudless and bright, and I found the remains of an ancient pastry in the bottom of a tote bag and fed the crumbs to a pigeon. Soon there were a dozen pigeons waddling around us, their feet leaving tracks in the sand in a cuneiform that I was not able to decode but I didn't care, and the water was cold on our toes and ankles, and Nina fell asleep in my arms on the way home, the train empty, the city finally quiet.

63

IT WAS COLD and my boots were torn, and of course I was lost. The sun was getting lower, and I knew it would be dark soon, so I hurried in the direction where I thought I'd seen a road. Mushrooms grew beneath the trees, and I tried to remember if they grew only on the north side like lichens, but I was pretty sure that was a myth, that lichens will grow anywhere. While I was pondering this I noticed a mouse running past. The mouse noticed me. It froze. Hello, I said. What are you doing here? You're the one that's lost, said the mouse. Is it that obvious? I asked. Oh well. I only meant that I thought you'd be hibernating. It's winter, after all. Is it? asked the mouse. The weather has been so topsy-turvy. Indeed, I agreed. Do you happen to know which way, I began to ask but then I realized that I wasn't lost because I didn't know the way to some specific place; I was lost because I didn't know where to go. You don't even know, do you? asked the mouse. I know lots of things, I said. But you don't know where you are, and you don't know where you're going, the mouse said. Correct, I said. And my feet are cold, and night is falling, and I'm lost alone in the woods, talking to a mouse. That's a very sad story, said the mouse. Perhaps, I said, but it's a story.

64

NINA DREW A snowstorm. It was not an ordinary snowstorm. It was blazing with color: green, red, purple, and orange lines filling the page to its margins. It's snow at Grandma's house, she said. And she had, in fact, been to my mother's place once in the snow, the only time she had ever seen the stuff. I didn't tell her, but it was sleet, really, barely an inch, and it melted within an hour. On a fresh page she drew summer. Summer summer summer, she said. She drew a heart, a star, a circle, sort of. It's not cold anymore, she said. Now it's nice and warm at Grandma's house, but she's not going to be there anymore.

65

THE MOON WAS a cartoon moon, a fat crescent hanging face-up in the sky, eye and nose in profile easy to make out. I was sitting in the rocking chair beside the Christmas tree. Maybe it was obvious that I was feeling sad. Nina ran up to me in her underwear and told me that people die, like grandma died, but you can see them in your dreams. So sleep, she said. I asked her for a hug. No, she said. Sleep. She took my hand and led me to the bedroom and showed me that she had laid out a pillow and a blanket for me on the floor beside a pile of oversized playing cards. These are hard pillows, she said, handing me a card with an image of a blue whale on its back. Here's a hard pillow so you can sleep and see people who died if you miss them. I took the card and thanked her, kissing her brow and holding her busy head in my hands for as long as she would let me, which wasn't long. I left the room and sat back down on the rocking chair, not even trying to hide my tears. Nina stood beside me, bouncing on her toes. Christmas tree! she shouted. It was only later that I noticed the moon.

66

I DREAMED THAT I was walking with my mother along a mountain pass. Sometimes it was so steep and rocky that I had to pick her up and carry her, but in the dream she was as light as Nina is, and she was her old self again: observant, interested in everything, happy to be with me in the world. Later I was walking with my sister through a strange and broken landscape. I don't know where our mother was. Instead of a house there were pieces of a house, whimsical surrealist stalactites protruding from the earth, fragments of clapboard, of couch, of fireplace, and kitchen. The next house we came to is already fading from my memory, but I think it was just rubble. Beyond that the land tilted sharply, all rock and scree, the footing difficult. We scrambled on, sliding as we went, aware of a precipice yawning a few feet ahead of us and to our left, if not bottomless then nearly so. There was a strange inevitability as we walked, talking calmly even as we slipped closer to the edge with each step, knowing that we would have to fight not to fall but also that it was coming no matter what we did. And then there it was, the very edge, and we tried to clamber up again but it was too late for that. The rocks were sliding away, all our efforts only bringing us closer until there was no more fighting, we had fallen, and I struggled not to scream and had the thought as I plummeted downward that this was it; I was going to fall for however long it took and then die when my body broke at the bottom, but I had this time left, these few seconds or fractions of seconds, and I shouldn't waste them with stupid fear but enjoy them—the hard chill of the wind on my neck, the whistling that it made, the rushing of my blood, the thump of my heart. Even thinking it, I knew this was a ridiculous thing to expect of myself. But still, I thought, how do you want to spend the rest of your life?

67

A LARGE PANTHER hides beneath a very small leaf. Really it is not hiding. It just has a leaf on its back. But it is darker than any shadow, and it counts on its coloring and its stillness to conceal it. The other animals are not fooled. It is clearly a panther. They avoid it, and, from a careful distance, laugh among themselves. It thinks it is hiding, they titter, covering their mouths, lest the glint of their teeth reveal them. Finally a monkey can't help itself. It descends halfway down a tree, still well out of the panther's reach, with plenty of room to race back into the canopy should it attack. You know we can all see you, the monkey says. You're not fooling anyone. The panther grins. Maybe you can see me, clever monkey, despite the leaf, but I am not afraid of you, and yet you and all your friends hide from me. I am hoping, the panther goes on, that if I can stay still enough, I will not see myself at all. But by then the monkey is gone, and the tree trunks and the vines—everything but the panther and the leaf.

68

NINA WANTED TO know about volcanoes, so I told her how they are just like mountains but they shoot fire that is actually molten rock, and if it touches you you'll die. Why? she said. I said something about pressure building up like in a pot of water on the stove, but she quickly lost interest in my explanation. Did Grandma die because of fire? she asked. No, I said. She died because she was old. I explained that you can die from a lot of things. You can die if a car hits you or a train hits you or if you fall from a high place or if you get very sick or if you can't swim and you fall in the sea or if you eat a bad mushroom or the wrong kind of berry. Or you can die if you're on fire, Nina added. Yes, I said, exactly. She thought about that for a while. We have to protect Grandma from fire, she concluded, so that she won't die again. I told her I agreed. Later she asked what Grandma looks like now. I couldn't answer that one. She didn't wait. Does anyone look funny when they die? she asked. Yes, I said. Most definitely.

69

I READ ABOUT Diane di Prima writing letters to a friend who had killed himself. She wrote one every day for a year. She would light a stick of incense and write until it burned away. About forty minutes, she said. That was in 1964. She had two small children, but perhaps people had more time in those days. I write on the bus and the metro—I often miss my stop—in the bathroom, on park benches, in coffee shops and restaurants, sometimes on the street, pausing to lean against a wall on my long walk home. Mainly I write sitting on the sofa in the brief window after Nina goes to sleep but before Livi and I do. Di Prima wrote that those forty minutes allowed her to "hold still." I imagine she was reading D.T. Suzuki and Alan Watts in those days, Zen a kind of touchstone in Beat circles. Incense required to shield mourning from the insults of the everyday. I'll never make it to a year, and the other passengers would complain if I lit a stick of incense here, the smoke threading between their tired legs and backpacks, the bus plunging on into the day.

70

LATER I WOULD take her in the wheelchair, but for some good part of the final years of my mother's life, I would walk with her as often as I could out to the wooden dock that reached into the river behind her apartment building. She would have gone every day if she could have, but often it was too cold or too hot or it was raining or I was rushed or I had Nina to look after and I would say, Sorry, Mama, maybe tomorrow. And when tomorrow came she would hobble down the hall to the elevator, dragging her cane like an unwanted limb, or, if I had won the argument, pushing her walker over the carpeted floors. On a bad day she would be exhausted by the time we made it down the long hall from the elevator to the building's front door, and sometimes we would barely make it outside before she would need to turn back, but usually her pride was stronger than her back or her legs or her pain on that particular day and she would push on through the parking lot and around the back. I would point out the birds to her as she shuffled onward, starlings and gulls and sometimes a heron on a piling, an eagle swooping low, an osprey frightening up a flock of panicked pigeons. Usually they were gone by the time she got around to looking. Eventually we would reach the foot of the dock, and I would try to convince her to walk down the middle so that I could follow behind her because I knew she preferred to teeter along at the edge with no guardrail to catch onto, just a weatherworn rope that hung limp between the pilings, and I would glance down to see how low the tide was and wonder how badly she'd get hurt if she fell and if I'd be able to carry her to shore through the sucking mud. I'd point out a cloud if there was a good towering altocumulus to be seen because I knew she had loved them once, and after a few steps I would take her arm and ignore her protests and walk beside her to the end of the pier and sit her down on the bench there, equally relieved and overcome with fresh dread at the thought of the walk back. But for a while, until her energy and attention flagged, we would sit out there, side by side, the sunlight warming her face, her eyes too cloudy and reflexes too slow to see the ospreys in their nests or whatever I was prattling on about, trying to distract you from your loneliness and all that had diminished you. And I was clouded, too, barely there, really, fighting back my own burning sadness as well as yours, sitting on the bench beside you but still stuck with you where we had been standing a few minutes ago, teetering at the edge of that old wooden dock, stumbling forward, and somehow, that time, anyway, managing not to fall.

71

SOMETIMES IN THE middle of the night and sometimes in the morning, sometimes not for months but sometimes twice or even three times in a single week, Nina wakes up laughing.

72

HOW LONG WILL it take to lose this nagging sensation that I need to call someone, that the one person I need to call is the one who can't be called? This nagging sensation that I've left something unfinished? This nagging sensation, even in the best of times, when joy floods in despite it all, that something is missing here, that something is fundamentally not right? Because something is missing, so much is gone missing, and I am surely not the only one who feels this way, and I suspect that, in fact, we are many. Mass delusion is a thing, of course, but if I am right, then perhaps we, all of us who feel this way, this silent and anonymous collective, are onto something and at least partly correct, because reality, so they say, is produced by consensus, which would mean that the universe, not just our sensations but whatever unites them, too, is unfinished and off-kilter, underdone and underbaked and not quite right, not right at all, and that we must call, all of us, somehow, right away, with urgency, on those who can't be called.

73

AT SOME POINT I will want to remember the lazy winter afternoon when Nina woke from her nap beside Livi and me on the narrow couch and she rolled on top of me, and she and I told Livi that we loved her, and Livi clowned and said, Me? You love *me*? with crazy eyes and then came over and buried us both in kisses, and Nina emitted a small tornado of giggles and rolled into her mother's arms, and from there they both told me that they loved me, and I clowned as if it couldn't be so and said, Me? You love *me*? I suppose my eyes were crazy too. I jumped on top of them and kissed their necks and bellies and cheeks as they laughed and laughed and whenever the storm of kisses seemed to flag, Nina would say it again, I love you, and I would kiss her all over her giant cheeks and ridiculous little chin and up and down her mama's neck and mouth, and then I would slow down again so that Nina would say it again. This also happened. Something like this happened all the time, every few days, even in the worst of it, and I will want to remember this, that this is what I meant when I explained to Nina that the oceans are liquid, that the sun is hot, that you can die by fire or in some slower fashion, that the moon will grow full and disappear and then grow full again, that spring follows winter just as winter follows fall, and that all living things want to be free.

74

THERE'S A HOLE in the moon that your heart fits in. There's a hole in my head that the breeze blows through. There's a hole in a tree where a tiger lives. Not that tiger, a different one. There's a hole in the sky where the stars should be. There's a hole in my chin where the light seeps out. There's a hole in each word where the meaning goes. There's a hole there's a hole there's a hole.

75

LIVI DIDN'T HAVE time to feed the chickens, so I said, Sure. I'll go. Just leave me the keys to the gate and the coop and remind me how much food to give them. Two bowls, she said. The sun was setting when I got there, the chickens hungry. They mobbed me when I stepped into the coop. I shut the door with care behind me, equally concerned that the chickens not get out and that I not, in my haste, lock myself in, as Livi had done a few weeks earlier. She had to shout for help, hoping some passerby would hear. The tourists all kept walking. She was rescued by a street sweeper. I emptied the first bowl of grain into the hanging feeder. The bigger birds shoved past the weaker ones. The rooster waited gallantly outside. He was young. More likely he was scared. I fetched the brush and dustpan from the storage bin, made a brief effort to scrape off the shit that had dried on the wire roost, then emptied another bowl of grain into the feeder. There was only one egg. In the springtime

Livi sometimes brings home eight or nine, but it was winter and they don't lay much when it's cold. I closed the door, locked the padlock, pulled the gate shut behind me, and walked home holding the cool egg in my hand. I made it almost to the corner before I noticed that my palm was wet. I could feel that the egg hadn't cracked. I couldn't understand it, but then I looked closely and saw, at the very center of the very top of the egg, a single perfect beak-sized hole.

77

I KNOW THE going wisdom is that stories are invested with a witchery stronger than death because they preserve our memories of a person and only memory can keep the dead alive. You would have been the first one to snort and say, What bullshit. That's not living. And you would be right, only that's not what stories do. They don't preserve anything. They create something new.

What I mean is that on the walk to Nina's nursery school I was a wolf. Every day we take on different shapes. Sometimes several times a day. Why do you have such a big mouth? Nina asked. The better to eat you with, I said on cue and gobbled at her neck. She giggled and thought about it. I wish Grandma had a big mouth, she said. Then she could be a wolf. She would like that, I said. I wish Grandma could see you right now, I said. That would make her very happy. For a moment the soft morning light felt sharp and blinding and every surface was a knife. The light was also a knife. For a moment I was gone. And it would make you very happy, Nina added. Yes, I said, recovering a little. It would.

78

I DIDN'T WRITE for two days. That's the story. Everything was fine. Everything was terrible. Wherever the words were is where they stayed. They didn't want me. Today everything is bathed in sadness. It's not in me, you see; it's outside of me. The street is slicked with it. The trees shiver with it. The sirens sing it, and the birds. The sun shines sorrow on the land. That's the story of today.

79

EVERYTHING IS FINE, really. I'm not complaining. It's just that I'm stuck here in this little submarine, or maybe it's a bathysphere, and I know that what I know is limited by what I am able to observe. What even is a bathysphere? I understand that it is storming outside but it's quiet in here and everything really is fine. In here you can't hardly feel it. Not the cold gusts but not the warm breezes either. And I wonder if this is what I am now, these walls. Stale air. No sense of where the surface is. If it's above or below. What if my outer layers, everything that separates me from the world, is not skin but a callus or a scab not made of human tissue. Who then can I be?

80

ON THE EVENING of Nina's first swimming lesson, I opened the door to the apartment and she charged me from the kitchen and jumped into my arms. Dada, she said, I went underwater!

81

WALKING THROUGH THE park I saw a magpie. It was so handsome, with its jet-black head, white shoulders, and long blue tail shimmering in the sun. You're gorgeous, I told it. A real looker. I mean it. Of course the magpie didn't answer. It already knew. It just pecked around in the dirt, looking for seeds or beetles or whatever it is that magpies eat. I know I'm ugly to you, I said, grotesque. I must look plucked. Like some dumb hairy worm stuck in the dirt of the earth. But I'm trying, you know. I'm writing this. That's not nothing, is it? The magpie spread its wings, fanning out an elegant shock of white before it took to the air. To my surprise it landed on my outstretched hand. It was heavier than it looked. Its eyes were circles inside circles. For a moment I thought I saw pity in them. I'm pretty sure I was projecting. Fly or don't fly, the magpie said. Fly if you want. And then it flew off, squawking. Stupid man, it said. Fly or don't.

82

THE BUS IS crowded in the evenings. People have to get home somehow. The sun must have set an hour ago, but the sky is glowing with the light from the streets and the buildings reflecting back down from the clouds. Funny how it can be brighter when it's dark. Things bounce more than you'd think they would. Cities are full of loud and inexplicable sounds, bangs and thumps and sirens. No one asks, What was that? It's the city. An ambulance proceeds slowly up my street, its lights flaring yellow and blue. A car parked on the corner flashes, too, but only yellow. It flickers on the brick wall of the pharmacy. People walk one way and another. Scooters race. The buildings keep their own counsel, crumbling slowly, secretly, in silence. All of it a script, a series of signs I do not know how to decipher. Does it matter? A breeze scares up two leaves and one sheet of crumpled paper. A car door shuts. Motorcycle police, more blue lights. Antennas. Bicycles. Bricks. The glint of a headlight reflected in a second-story window and then, just as suddenly, gone. A dead plant in a pot in a dim building lobby. A woman pulled along by two dogs. Taxis always in a hurry.

83

IT WAS WINDY this morning. Maybe everyone will blow away, Nina said as we walked out the door to the street. She didn't seem worried. Later when I got off the bus, heading home from the office, the palm trees on the boulevard were lit from behind, their fronds gilded by the sinking sun. I stood on the sidewalk and watched them, whipped by the wind, dancing.

84

DOES A STORY have to end?

85

LIVI BROUGHT THE balloon to the restaurant. It was easily a meter tall, a glistening greenish blue in the shape of the number three, tethered by two purple cords to a weight wrapped in purple mylar. It bobbed beside the table as we ate, a silent if impatient companion. I carried it back to the office under my arm, wrestling with it when the wind rose up and it fought to get away. On the bus on my way home, all the children stared up at it from their strollers in an ecstasy of envy. When Nina came home and found it in her bedroom she fell on her knees. "Ballooooon!" she howled. It was love. It was her birthday. After her bath she danced with it on the top rung of the stepladder, the three's bottom arc hooked around her waist like a lover's arm. Early the next morning, I looped its cords around my wrist and walked it to the park to claim a table. When the wind gusted hard, the mylar-wrapped weight wasn't enough to hold it down so I lay a backpack filled

76

I ASKED NINA if she had ever eaten a duck. I knew the answer, of course. I was just making conversation. She said no, and I told her that ducks taste very good, which is too bad for them. Why? she asked. Why is it bad? Because ducks don't want to be eaten, I said. Why? she asked. Because they want to be alive, I said. Why? she asked. Because living things want to be alive, I said. Why? she asked, relentless. Do you want to be alive? I asked. Yes, she answered, and thought for a moment. But why? she asked. Because life is beautiful, I said. She thought about that too. But sometimes life is not beautiful, she said. It was my turn to think for a moment. I was surprised, of course. She's not yet three. I didn't know how to respond. I wanted to tell her, and perhaps myself, that sometimes it hurts so much that we can't see it, but that beauty and pain or even ugliness are hardly opposites. But that seemed too complicated and contradictory a thought to convey with her perched on my shoulders like a prince riding an elephant as I climbed the endless concrete steps up the hillside to her nursery school, so I agreed with her. That's true, I said. Sometimes it is difficult and painful. And sometimes, she added, life is merry-go-round-y. And though I couldn't see her face, I knew there was brightness in her eyes, delight at the word she had invented and at the thought of it, all those colorful horses and cars, motorcycles and rocket ships, circling and rising up and down, always the same cheerful song.

with bottled juice and soda over it to prevent it from flying off. Later, Livi and Nina arrived, pushing the birthday cake in Nina's stroller. One kid came and then another kid and another. Their parents came with them. We struggled to light the candles and keep them lit, and we sang in a hurry so that Nina could blow them out before the wind did. Then the sun dropped behind the trees, and we piled everything into the strollers and made for a warmer and less shady corner of the park, closer to the playground. I was chatting with Alessandro by the seesaw when suddenly he looked up with something like awe in his eyes, as if the Virgin had appeared in the sky above the city. Or maybe Mothra. I followed his gaze. Oh no. There it was, sparkling bright against the blue of the sky as the wind took it over the park. Nina, on the low end of the seesaw, saw it, too, and I heard her cry out in agony behind me as I dashed after it, not pausing to doubt or laugh at myself, stupid man, for chasing a thing that could fly, and I jumped down the steps and raced out of the park and kept running into the streets while it rose above the trees, over the fence and the avenue and the high-rises beyond it, up and up until it was finally out of my sight, gleaming, gone, free.

"Blow," "A boy dies," and
"See the sea," were written on the days that
Carmen Landau, Qusai Mahmoud al-Tamimi,
and Mike Davis died, or on the days that
I learned of their deaths. RIP.